Walrus's Gift

BY

H.E. Stewart

Library and Archives Canada Cataloguing in Publication

Stewart, H. E. (Helen Elizabeth), 1943-

Walrus's gift : making friends / H.E. Stewart.

ISBN 978-0-9693852-7-1

I. Title.

PS8587.T4855W35 2011   jC813'.54   C2010-908008-4

Manufactured by Friesens Corporation in
Altona, Manitoba, in January 2011, Job #61809

PRINTED IN CANADA

Tudor House Press is committed to reducing the consumption of ancient forests.
This book is one step towards that goal. It is printed on acid-free paper that is
100% ancient forest free, and has been processed chlorine free.

TUDOR
HOUSE
PRESS

for my son Toby,

who is as kind-hearted as the walrus in this story

Sometimes a picture is not what it seems to be.

In this picture, a young boy looks out upon a beautiful ocean. At first glance, this is a peaceful image. But look more closely and you will see that the boy appears to be sad. Each day he sits alone, watching the water.

A young walrus happens to swim nearby.
He watches and wonders why the boy is always
alone and how he could be sad when the ocean
is so filled with such different and interesting life.

He asks his mother why the boy might be unhappy. She does not know about people children, but she does know about walrus children, especially her own watchful son. She suggests that he ask Grandfather who is older and knows more of the world. Grandfather, after all, has listened to many stories over many long years.

So the young walrus swims off happily to find his grandfather – who pays full attention to the problem, recognizing the little walrus's concern and his kind heart. Grandfather considers the question carefully.

He decides to give the little walrus an important and unusual present – a special seashell that carries the sound of the ocean, a shell that also carries other voices. If the walrus child listens very closely, he will be able to hear and better understand the boy child.

And this is how the young walrus learns why the boy is sad and lonely. He is left out because he is quiet and does not play games. With curly, carrot-coloured hair, he even looks different. He definitely does not fit in with the others.

The people children all try to be like one another, so they make fun of anyone who is in any way different. And because they copy one another's behaviour, they all tease the same child – without thinking too much about what they are doing.

Why do they do this? Where ever do they learn to act like this?

The kind-hearted young walrus feels sorry for the boy. He returns to Grandfather to tell him about what he has seen and heard. Once again, Grandfather listens carefully. But this time even Grandfather does not know what to do. He is old and wise enough, however, to know that everyone helping is often better than just one working alone.

This is a problem calling for many ideas and suggestions – a problem calling for a gathering of the sea creatures. At such a gathering, any creature is allowed to speak and all the others will listen – for any one of them, great or small, may have a valuable contribution to make.

Grandfather considers it important for the young walrus to befriend the boy child and talk with him. Dolphin wisely suggests that the walrus child watch the other children and speak with them as well. Playful Otter has the idea that the young walrus will need a disguise in order to go to school.

Now clever Raven is quick to offer his help. This is just the job for him. Surely he can think of a way to dress up the walrus child. Immediately he sets off, flying about the countryside, searching hither and yon, taking what is necessary from here and there.

When Raven has collected all that he needs, he is ready to perform his trick. With a bit of magic – and a bit of help from his friends – he stuffs the young walrus into the people child clothes.

Now the young walrus is ready to go to school. But what should he do once he gets there? What should he say to the boy child?

A long discussion follows. At last the sea creatures all agree on a plan, and only then is the walrus child ready to set off on his mission.

When he arrives at the school, he first finds the lonely boy and makes friends with him. Before long he tells the boy all about the sea animals and their ideas.

He explains about teasing (which often leads to bullying) and tells the boy what the sea creatures think should be done. He suggests the boy should walk away when someone is making fun of him and try to ignore the teasing. The boy explains that this is what he has been doing and this is why he is always alone. Walrus says perhaps then he should try talking with the people children – and if that is too difficult, he must talk with someone else. It is most important that he tell someone about his problems, otherwise no one will know that he needs help. He must seek help from a teacher or another adult.

By now the other children notice the walrus child speaking with the boy. They are surprised that the boy has such an unusual visitor. Drawn by curiosity, they gather closer to see what is happening. When they overhear what the walrus child is saying, they are even more surprised – and for the first time, they begin to think about their own behaviour.

Their thoughts are interrupted when the bell rings and they must return (very reluctantly) to their classroom. The walrus child is left alone to make his way back to the ocean and the sea creatures who are waiting for him.

The sea animals are very proud of the young walrus child. They are proud of him for paying attention and for noticing the boy child and then wanting to help. They are pleased that he had the courage to talk with the boy.

After cheers for the little walrus, another discussion begins. Now the sea creatures decide that the walrus child should return one more time to the school with one more important message for the boy.

The very next morning the young walrus cheerfully sets off once again. He soon finds the boy and learns that he has talked with his teacher – who did pay attention. And the teacher talked with the children. And there seems to have been some change, for the boy is a bit happier.

The little walrus delivers one last suggestion from the sea creatures – the boy must try to look inside himself for strength and courage when he feels left out. After all, he has done nothing wrong, nothing to deserve teasing. He is a special child, as is every child. He has his own talents to contribute. And besides, how many children are there who have a walrus for a friend?

It is important that the boy also learn to think for himself. Then one day he may be able to help someone else who is feeling left out. And the walrus child has provided a perfect example for the boy child to follow.

Walrus's Gift is in some ways like a native legend. It speaks of the wisdom of elders, of co-operation among the community, and of a search for individual inner strength.

Animals have always been an important part of native culture. They appear often in stories and legends with characteristics that are relevant to the story of *Walrus's Gift*.

Dolphin

Dolphin is the keeper of the power of sacred breath and a protector of the weak. Dolphins have long been associated with humans.

Otter

Otter is a symbol of joy, playfulness and sharing.

Eagle

Eagle represents the power of the Great Spirit, courage, order and harmony. Eagle down is still used as an expression of welcoming friendship.

Raven

Raven is a creator and guardian of magic. He is also a messenger and a trickster, capable of mystical transformation.

Heron

Heron exemplifies self-reliance and inner strength.

Loon

Loon stands for imagination and the re-awakening of old hopes and dreams.

Kingfisher

Kingfisher represents patience, skill, vision and a concern for community.

Salmon

Salmon are a symbol of life, of courage and strength, as well as respect for tradition.

The idea of a walrus talking to children about bullying was thought up by policeman Tom Woods.

His work eventually grew into the WITS (Walk away, Ignore, Talk it out, Seek help) Program, designed to alleviate teasing and bullying in elementary schools. This program was developed by Bonnie Leadbeater, PhD, Professor of Psychology at the University of Victoria. It is supported by the Rock Solid Foundation. For more information and teacher guidelines, please visit www.witsprogram.ca